First published in Belgium and Holland by Clavis Uitgeverij, Hasselt – Amsterdam, 2009
2009, Clavis Uitgeverij

English translation from the Dutch by Clavis Publishing Inc. New York
Copyright © 2010 for the English language edition: Clavis Publishing Inc. New York

Visit us on the web at www.clavisbooks.com

Copyright © 2009 Leo Timmers
*Crow* written and illustrated by Leo Timmers
Original title: *Kraai*
Translated from the Dutch by Clavis Publishing

ISBN 978-1-60537-071-2

This book was printed in June 2010 at Drukarnia Legra Sp z.o.o, 30-716 Krakow, Poland

First Edition
10 9 8 7 6 5 4 3 2 1

# Crow

Leo Timmers

Clavis

**NEW YORK**

Crow used to be alone all the time.
All the birds avoided him.
"What's wrong with me?" Crow cawed.

One day he heard loud chirping sounds.
It was jolly. And close.

What a cheerful flock, Crow thought.
"Hello ..." he said softly, but they didn't hear him.

With his friendliest smile, Crow tiptoed towards them.

They were scared to death when Crow suddenly appeared
beside them!
With pounding hearts, they flew away in all directions.

At a safe distance, they started chirping again.

"Black!" Finch squeaked. "He's pitch-black from top to toe."

"Not even a touch of color," Parakeet gaggled.

"He's not to be trusted."

"Brrr," Chickadee shivered. "Must be a mean creature."

Crow heard everything.
Never before had he felt so black.
"I'm a creep," he moaned.
"A scarecrow of tar and feathers.
I wish I was different. I wish I was ..."
Of course, that's it!
Suddenly, Crow knew what to do.

Crow rushed around to gather everything he needed.

"No one will be afraid of me any more,"
Crow laughed mysteriously.
Immediately, he got to work.
When he was ready, it seemed like a miracle had happened.

Crow turned into a finch!

Then he turned into a parakeet.

And into a chickadee ...

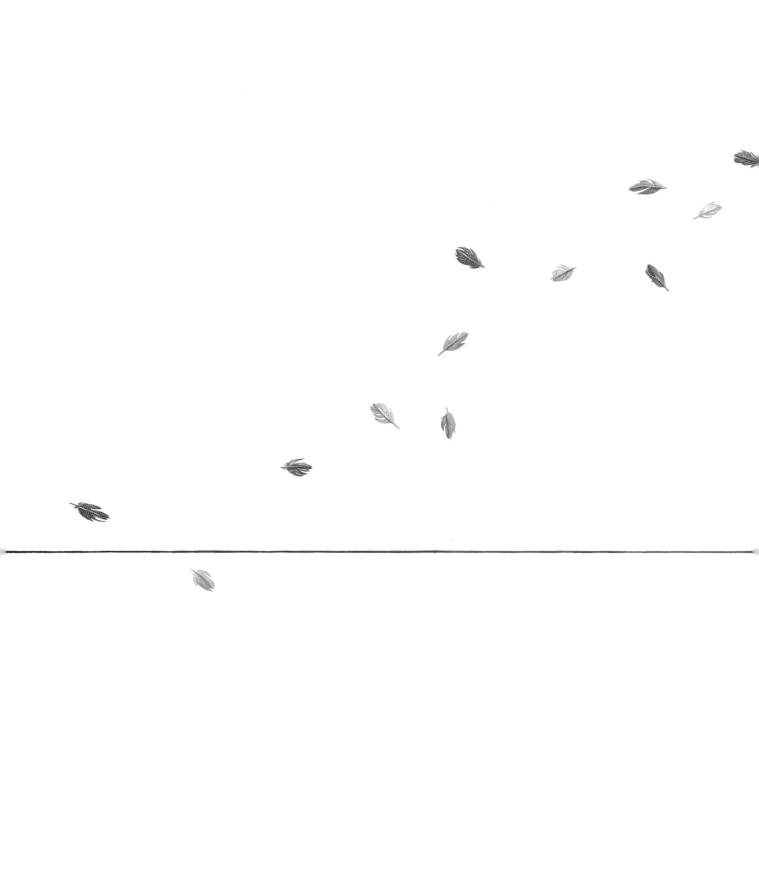

"It doesn't work," Crow cried.
"What do I have to do?"
Big, wet tears ran down his feathers.
All his colors dripped to the ground.
He was black again. As black as ...
"Mister Crow?"
Crow heard a little voice.
An anxious little voice.

There they were again, all three of them!
"Are they gone?" Chickadee squeaked.
"Gone?" Crow stammered. "Who?"

"That hideous chickadee, that scary parakeet and
that creepy finch, of course!" they screamed with one voice.
"Err ... yes, they are," Crow nodded.
"They are gone and they will never come back."
"I knew it!" Finch sang. "You have scared them away with
your burly black beak and your dark feathers."
"Hurray!" Parakeet cheered. "Crow has saved us!"

Crow glittered with pride.
He was so proud he didn't dare to tell his new friends
what had really happened.
He would tell them later.

Maybe ...